Words to Know Before You Read

farmer

me

patch

then

veggies

who

www.rourkeeducationalmedia.com

Edited by Luana Mitten
Illustrated by Jenny Snape
Art Direction and Page Layout by Renee Brady

Library of Congress PCN Data

Who Stole the Veggies from the Veggie Patch? / Precious McKenzie
ISBN 978-1-61810-165-5 (hard cover) (alk. paper)
ISBN 978-1-61810-298-0 (soft cover)
Library of Congress Control Number: 2012936767

Rourke Educational Media
Printed in the United States of America,
North Mankato, Minnesota

Also Available as:

rourkeeducationalmedia.com

customerservice@rourkeeducationalmedia.com • PO Box 643328 Vero Beach, Florida 32964

Who Stole the Veggies from the Veggie Patch?

By Precious McKenzie
Illustrated by Jenny Snape

Rabbit stole the radishes
from the veggie patch.

Not me! Wasn't me!

Possum stole the peas
from the veggie patch.

Who, me?
Yes, you!

Not me! Wasn't me!

10

Then who?

11

Coyote stole the carrots
from the veggie patch.

Who, me?
Yes, you!

13

Not me! Wasn't me!

Lamb stole the lettuce
from the veggie patch.

Who, me?
Yes, you!

17

18

Then who?

19

Farmer stole the veggies from the veggie patch!

After Reading Activities

You and the Story...

What went missing from the veggie patch?

How many animals were accused of stealing the veggies from the veggie patch?

Did the ending surprise you?

What is going to happen to all of the veggies?

Do you like to eat veggies?

Words You Know Now...

Can you find a word with a short e sound like set?
Can you find a word with a long e sound like beat?

farmer   then

me   veggies

patch   who

You Could...Play Who Stole The Veggies From The Veggie Patch?

- Ask several friends to take turns repeating the story.

- Decide who goes first, second, third, fourth, and so on.

- As you go around the group, insert the person's name where the animal's name was.

- Then work your way backward through the group, repeating all of the lines from the story.

- See how long you can keep this game going!

About the Author

Precious McKenzie loves to watch animals sneak into her garden. Precious lives with her husband and three children in Montana.

Meet The Author!
www.meetREMauthors.com

About the Illustrator

Jenny Snape grew up in the north of England. She has loved to draw since she was a little girl, especially animals and people. Jenny now lives in London with her husband and enjoys walking her dog, Tony, every day in the park.